Level 1 is ideal for children who have received some initial reading instruction. Each story is told very simply, using a small number of frequently repeated words.

Special features:

Opening pages introduce key story words

The grass

The bridge

The first billy goat Gruff

The second billy goat Gruff

The troll

The third billy goat Gruff

6

7

Careful match between story and pictures

"I'm hungry," said the first billy goat Gruff. "I'm going over the bridge to eat the grass."

Large, clear type

8

9

Educational Consultant: Geraldine Taylor
Book Banding Consultant: Kate Ruttle

A catalogue record for this book is available from the British Library

Published by Ladybird Books Ltd
80 Strand, London, WC2R 0RL
A Penguin Company

009

ISBN: 978-0-72327-275-5

Printed in China

The Three
Billy Goats Gruff

Illustrated by Richard Johnson

The first billy
goat Gruff

The second billy
goat Gruff

The third billy goat Gruff

The grass

The bridge

The troll

"I'm hungry," said the
first billy goat Gruff.
"I'm going over the
bridge to eat the grass."

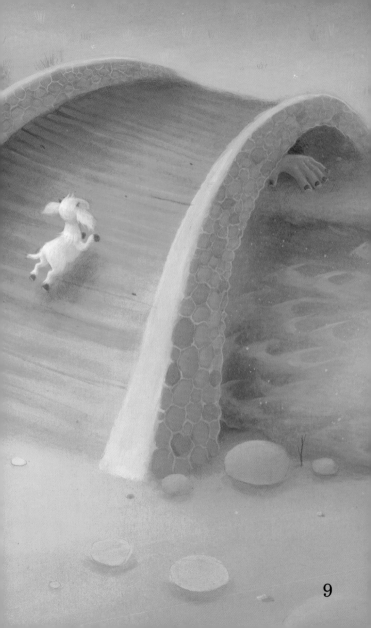

Trip, trap!

Trip, trap!

Trip, trap!

11

Up jumped the troll.

"I'm going to eat you up,"
said the troll.

"Oh no," said the
first billy goat Gruff.
"Don't eat me. Eat the
second billy goat Gruff.
He's big and fat."

15

"I'm hungry," said the second billy goat Gruff. "I'm going over the bridge to eat the grass."

Trip, trap!

Trip, trap!

Trip, trap!

Up jumped the troll.

"I'm going to eat you up," said the troll.

19

"Oh no," said the second billy goat Gruff. "Don't eat me. Eat the third billy goat Gruff. He's big and fat."

"I'm hungry," said the third billy goat Gruff. "I'm going over the bridge to eat the grass."

Trip, trap!

Trip, trap!

Trip, trap!

23

Up jumped the troll.

"I'm going to eat you up," said the troll.

"Oh no you're not," said the third billy goat Gruff. "I'm going to eat YOU up."

And that was the end of the troll!

How much do you remember about the story of The Three Billy Goats Gruff? Answer these questions and find out!

- Why do the three billy goats Gruff want to go over the bridge?

- Where does the troll live?

- What does the troll want to do to the three billy goats Gruff?

To
HARPER,

From

....

You may have heard the stories?
I tell you they are true!
A superhero lives nearby.
But where? I wish I knew!

She's got an "H" upon her suit,
Her cape is long and flowing.

Who is the girl behind the mask?
There's just no way of knowing!

Oh no! A cat's stuck up a tree!
But who will get it out?
Our hero stops and says,
                    "I'll use my...

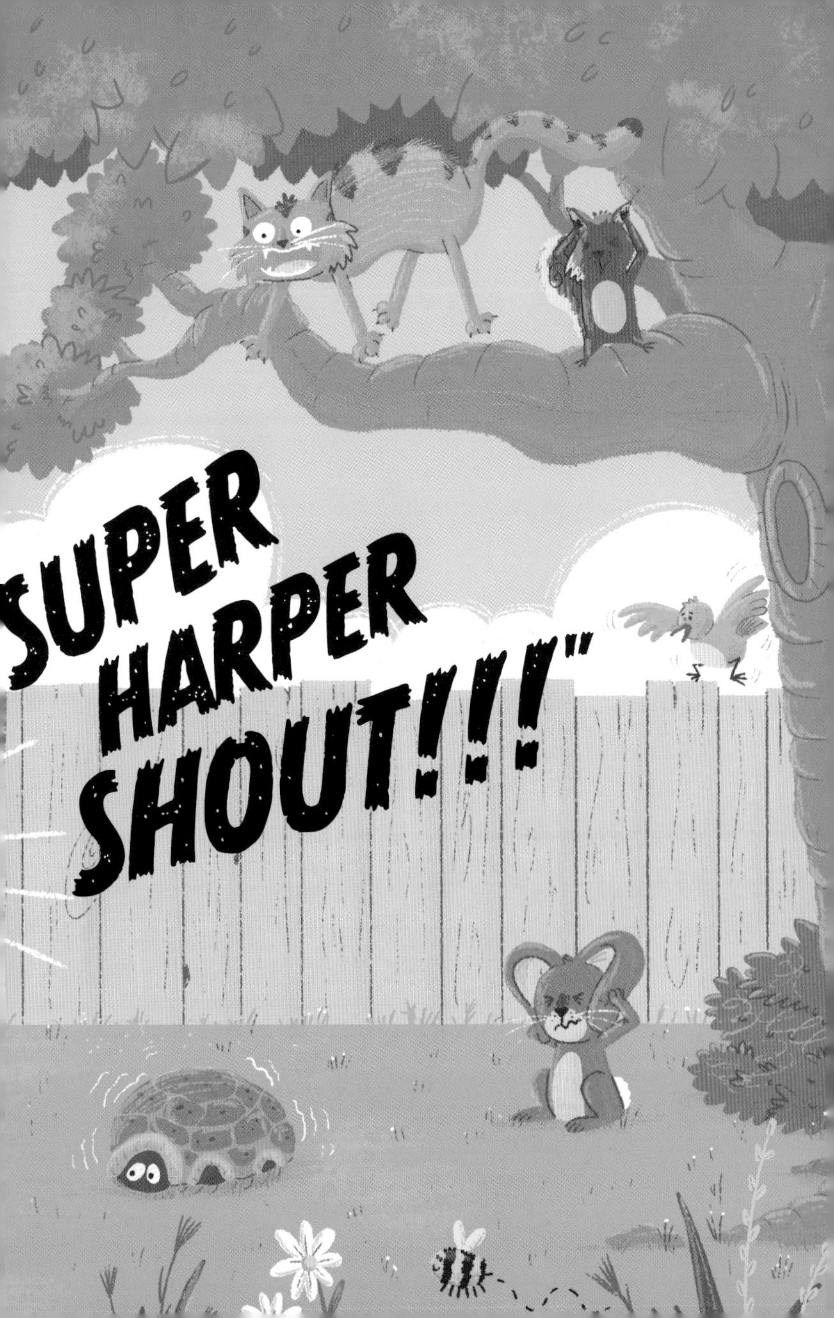
SUPER
HARPER
SHOUT!!!"

This little girl is crying.
Her trike has got a flat.

I guess it must be hungry work
When one is fighting crime.
She runs and jumps and dives around.
She's moving all the time!

Super Harper is so strong,
She simply can't be beaten.
It must be all the salad, sprouts,
And broccoli she's eaten!

There's trouble on the playground!
Kids start to scream and shout.

Super Harper, kind and true,
Knows how to work this out!

Uh-oh! That child's about to fall.
He'll get a nasty scrape!

But never fear,
For guess who's here?
Our hero in a cape!

She's the world's best superhero.
And she's got a super cuddle!

The next time you're in trouble,
Or ever in harm's way, shout. . .

This superhero stuff's hard work,
And now she's very sleepy,
But Super Harper feels afraid–
Her bedroom looks so creepy!

Yet heroes do not run or hide
When they are feeling scared!
Instead they face their fears head on.
That's why she's come prepared!

She's caring and she's helpful,
Always doing awesome deeds.
Yes, Super Harper is the hero
Everybody needs!

She's always super-wonderful.
She's super-terrific, too.
Just who is Super Harper?
WAIT! I think it must be. . .

Written by Eric James
Illustrated by Steve Brown
Designed by Ryan Dunn

Copyright © Hometown World Ltd 2018

Put Me In The Story is a
registered trademark of Sourcebooks, Inc.
All rights reserved.

Published by Put Me In The Story,
a publication of Sourcebooks, Inc.
P.O. Box 4410, Naperville, Illinois 60567-4410
(630) 961-3900
www.putmeinthestory.com

Date of Production: October 2018
Run Number: HTW_PO201833
Printed and bound in Italy (LG)
10 9 8 7 6 5 4 3 2 1

put me
in the story®
Bestselling books starring your child!
www.putmeinthestory.com